What Lola Wants... Lola Gets

With dazzling 3D animation
using Augmented Reality technology

by
David Salariya

Illustrated by
Carolyn Scrace

Scribblers
A Division of Book House

Hello, darlings,

I am Lola.

I am purrrrrr fect.

This is Monty.

He is not quite Purrrrrr fect.

Wobble

Oh no, Monty!

Reclining for grooming,
I cannot resist.
It takes time to be purrrrrr fect.

Monty tries his best,
but his idea of style
is less than
purrrrrr fect.

Oh no, Monty!

Scrub and scrub

To be picture purrrr fect
is my dream.

Monty tries his best,
but his skills are
less than Purrrrrr fect.

Delicate nibbles I long for.
Scrumptious dishes
I adore.

Wobble

Monty tries his best
to please me, but his
cooking is less
than purrrrrr fect.

Monty tries his best
at driving... but on two wheels?
I think you must agree,
the results are less than

purrrrrr fect.

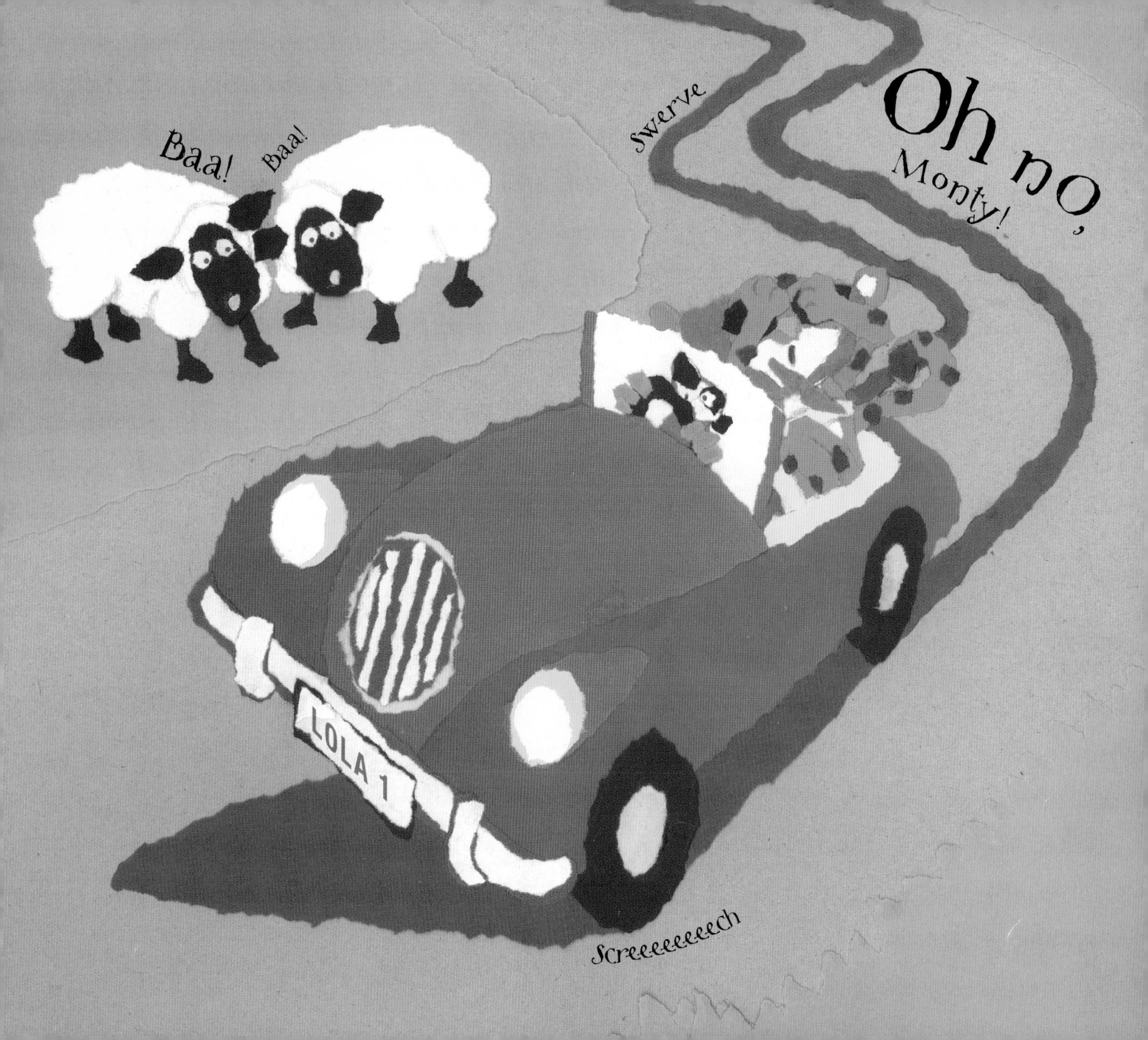

Baa!
Baa!
Swerve
Oh no,
Monty!
LOLA 1
Screeeeeeeech

Stunning flowers I'd adore, with hedges
clipped to perfection. Monty tries his best
but as you must agree, the results are
less than **PURRRRR**fect.

Snip

Oh no, Monty!

Monty tries his best at dusting, but the results are less than **purrrrr**fect.

Oh no, Monty!

Crash

You ask, darlings,
'Is Monty purrrrrr fect
at anything?'

Oh YES, Monty!

Oh Monty, you are... purrrrrr fect!